Krystal Ball is published by Picture Window Books,
a Capstone imprint
1710 Roe Crest Drive
North Mankato, Minnesota 56003
www.capstoneyoungreaders.com

Cataloging-in-Publication Data is available on the Library
of Congress website.
ISBN: 978-1-4795-5874-2 (library hardcover)
ISBN: 978-1-4795-5876-6 (paperback)
ISBN: 978-1-4795-6197-1 (eBook)

Summary: It's the annual school bake-off, and Krystal Ball
is making fortune cookies, of course! Will the cookies
lead to a sweet victory, or will the competition leave
Krystal sour? Find out in this adventure of Krystal Ball,
fourth-grade fortune-teller.

Designer: Kay Fraser

Printed in China.
092014 008472RRDS15

Krystal Ball

FORTUNE COOKIE FIASCO

by Ruby Ann Phillips
illustrated by Sernur Isik

PICTURE WINDOW BOOKS

Table of Contents

My Future Awaits

Hi there! My name is Krystal Ball. I'm from Queens, which is a part of New York City. Some people call this place the Big Apple. But I live in a tiny, two-bedroom apartment with my mom and dad, so it seems pretty small to me.

Don't get me wrong . . . I *love* my parents. My mom works as a hair stylist on the first floor of our building. My dad's a high school history teacher. He's always saying things like, "History repeats itself, sweetie." Whatever that means.

I'm not that interested in the past, though. I'm much more excited about . . . the future.

I like astrology, palm reading, and stargazing. Why? Well, let me tell you a little secret. I'm not exactly normal. I may look small, you see, but I'm really a medium. That means I have a special ability, kind of like a sixth sense. My grandma calls this my "gift." It helps me see what the future holds, but it's never quite clear. I can learn things about a person or an object by touching them, and sometimes my dreams show little glimpses of events that haven't happened yet.

I usually have trouble understanding these visions, or premonitions, but I'm working on improving my skills. I also go to Nikola Tesla Elementary School, and being a fourth-grade fortune-teller while juggling science projects, math tests, and homework isn't easy.

What else can I tell you about me? Ah! My best friend, Billy, lives in the apartment above ours. I've known him my whole life, and that's a really long time. Almost ten years . . . Whoa! My other best friend, Claire, is the new girl at school. Both Billy and Claire know about my amazing gift, but they have pinky-sworn to secrecy.

Together, we zip around the neighborhood on our scooters, seeking out adventure. But with my abilities, adventure usually finds us first!

Okay, so you got all that? Good.

Now take a deep breath, relax your eyes, and clear your mind. My future awaits . . .

CHAPTER 1

Mean Team

RECESS! My favorite time of day at Nikola Tesla Elementary School. And this recess was like most others. The sun was shining, and my friends and I were running around the playground.

Only this time . . . I was running for my life!

"Slow down, so that I may eat your brains!" cried my best friend, Billy Katsikis.

"Please, no!" I shouted back. "Anything but my sweet, delicious brains."

I ran faster across a stretch of field, but Billy was gaining on me. "BRAINS!" he screamed.

"Stop, brain breath!" commanded a voice.

I whirled around to see my other best friend, Claire Voyance. She stood firmly in place with her hands on her hips.

Billy licked his lips and rubbed his hands. "Mmm . . . *More* delicious brains for me to eat!"

"I don't think so," answered Claire. She pointed a ruler at Billy and said, "ZAP!"

Billy froze in place. Then he started to shake as if shocking energy were coursing through his body.

"Blast you!" he cried.

"No," I corrected. "Blast *you*! Back to the Nether Region."

"Aaaaaarrrgh!" Billy shouted, and he crumpled to the ground in a heap.

Claire and I high-fived and laughed.

You see, I wasn't really in danger. My friends and I were playing a game called Paranormal Investigators. We pretend to be a team of detectives that hunt down ghosts, goblins, and other spooks. We find them and zap them back to their original dimension.

Cool, huh?

As we helped Billy off the ground, I started to get a vision. I shut my eyes and tilted my head. I felt as if cold, icy fingers were tapping my spine.

"Do you see something?" added Billy.

I shivered and opened my eyes. "I didn't see anything," I said, "but I have a feeling that something bad is going to happen."

TWEET! At that moment, the recess monitor blew her whistle. It was time to go back inside.

"See, that's all it was," said Claire. "You foresaw the end of recess. A *very* bad thing."

I smiled, but deep down I knew that the results of my powers were never that simple.

"Ugh," Billy said, pointing behind us. "Don't look now, but something wicked is coming."

Sashaying our way were Kate, Susan, and Emily. Or, as we called them, the Mean Team. These girls turned their noses up at you if you didn't wear the latest fashions, have the latest hairstyle, or carry the latest designer bag.

I didn't register on their radar at all.

"Hi, Krystal," Kate said sweetly.

She was definitely up to something.

"Did you enjoy recess?" she asked, batting her fake pageant-queen eyelashes.

The question seemed simple enough, but I was starting to sweat. A crowd gathered around us. My throat was dry and scratchy.

"Um . . . yes," I managed to say.

"Oh, good." Kate responded. "The girls and I were worried you were going to get your brains eaten by the Hungry Hippo over here."

She pointed to Billy and erupted into laughter. Susan and Emily cackled with her.

"The whole class saw you running around like crazy people," Kate continued.

Now my face was red. If I were a cartoon, steam would have been shooting out of my ears.

"Listen here!" Claire snapped.

A hushed silence fell over the crowd.

"If Billy really did eat brains," said Claire, "*you* would have nothing to worry about!"

Somebody gasped with shock.

I turned to look at Claire. She was furious, and I was dumbstruck. Claire is usually really quiet and shy, but right now she was Wonder Woman.

"Excuse me?" Kate shrilled.

Claire took a step forward. "You heard me."

Kate took a step back.

This time Billy spoke up. "Of course you don't understand us," he said. "We don't speak *lame brain* fluently like you do."

Some of the other kids started to chuckle. The recess monitor was making her way over to us.

I grabbed Billy and Claire and dragged them into the school. We ran until we got to our classroom and sat in our desks.

"Did that just happen?" I asked, panting. "You were amazing. I can't believe you actually stood up to Kate."

"Believe it, sister," Claire said. She was flushed. "Grr! Those brats get right under my skin."

At that moment, Kate, Susan, and Emily walked into the room.

They glared at us, flipped their hair in unison, and stomped to their desks in a huff.

"Settle down class," Miss Callisto said. "I've got a special announcement to make."

Suddenly, my body started to tingle. I shut my eyes and tilted my head.

Billy and Claire looked over at me.

A fuzzy feeling washed over me that made me forget all about Kate and the Mean Team. Being a medium certainly had its advantages.

I opened my eyes and said, "Outlook good!"

CHAPTER 2

Bake-Off!

Miss Callisto clapped her hands together to get our attention. "The annual Nikola Tesla Elementary School Bake-Off is upon us," she exclaimed. "It's a fund-raiser for the school, and our class is going to participate!"

"Mmm . . . bake-off," Billy said. His family owned a bakery called the House of Sweets, so Billy knew a little about baking. But he knew *a lot* about eating.

"I'll divide the class into groups," Miss Callisto said. "Each group will be responsible for one baked good to sell on the day of the event.

"Aaaaaaand," she added, building suspense, "the group with the best dessert will win a trip to the Bronx Zoo!"

The class buzzed with excitement.

Billy had a dreamy look on his face, and I was certain he had visions of sugarplums dancing in his head.

"Mmm . . . baked goods." He drooled.

Miss Callisto went around the room assigning groups. She said that Claire, Billy, and I were in a group together. Yay!

"What should we make?" Claire asked us both.

"So many choices . . ." Billy began. "Cupcakes, cookies, marshmallow squares, fruit turnovers, chocolate croissants, and tea biscuits with fillings and icings and toppings galore!"

I was just as giddy. I'd always dreamed of going to the Bronx Zoo!

"Together we'll come up with something," I said. "Or maybe the universe will tell me."

I closed my eyes and put my index fingers to my temples.

"And what disgusting treats are you dreaming up, Krystal," said a voice. "Baked brains?"

I opened my eyes and spotted the Mean Team.

"Baked brains!" Susan repeated, pinching her nose. "Ewwww!"

"Good one," Emily said with a laugh.

I hoped that if I ignored them, they would just go away. Claire had other plans.

"I see you're back for round two," she said, folding her arms. "Bring it, blondie!"

At that moment, the bell rang.

"Class dismissed," called Miss Callisto. "See you tomorrow."

Claire smirked and said, "Saved by the bell."

Kate stuck out her tongue and walked away. Susan and Emily followed.

I breathed a sigh of relief. The worst was over. "You're much braver than I am," I said. "Whenever Hurricane Kate blows through, I just want to run for cover."

"Ha!" Billy bellowed. "Hurricane Kate! Now that's a good one."

Claire and I chuckled.

* * *

Later that afternoon, I was sitting in the kitchen with my mother doing homework. The hair salon was closed for the day, and Dad was still at his school grading papers.

Mom was helping me memorize the fifty US states and their capitals. It felt like we'd been studying for hours!

"Can I please take a break now, Mom?" I pleaded. "My brain is fried!"

I tugged on a handful of my curls and pulled them up high over my head.

"Look at the smoke coming out of it!" I said.

Mom smiled, trying not to laugh.

"Honey, you're doing great," she said. "We're almost done!"

"I'm already done," I said. "Stick a fork in me!"

This time, Mom laughed out loud.

Just then, the door opened and Dad walked in.

"Daddy, you're home!" I jumped out of my seat and ran to hug him.

"Hmm," Dad said, looking me in the eyes. "I don't have to be psychic to see that something is bothering you."

I nodded, and I told my parents about Kate and the Mean Team and what happened at recess.

"Oh, honey," my mother said. "Is there anything we can do to help?"

"No," I moaned. "It's all hopeless!"

Dad rubbed his chin. He always did this when he was thinking.

"I have an idea," he said. "Put on your coats. I'm taking you out for dinner tonight."

"Ooh!" I exclaimed. My spirits suddenly lifted. "Where? Tell me."

"Better not tell you now," Dad said, teasing me. "It's a surprise."

"I love surprises!" I cheered.

CHAPTER 3

Good Fortune

"Marvelous moonbeams!" I exclaimed, running into my bedroom. "A surprise! I must put on something more fashionable."

In an instant, I became a whirlwind of wardrobe changes. Scarves and skirts and shirts and shawls came flying out of my closet. Nothing I tried on looked right.

Suddenly, I got a buzzing feeling inside my brain. I closed my eyes and tilted my head.

Then an image appeared. It was Grandma, and she was standing on the Great Wall of China.

"Eureka!" I cried aloud. I knew exactly what I was going to wear.

You see, Grandma had recently gone on a trip to China and visited many temples and ruins and wonders, like the Great Wall.

When she came back, she brought me this wonderful silver vest made of silk. On it was an ornamental gardenia pattern. (FYI: Gardenias are my favorite flower. They're Grandma's too!)

Once I found the vest in my closet, I held it up and watched the light shimmer off the fabric.

I put the vest on over a black button-down blouse and black slacks.

Hmm . . . needs a splash of color, I thought.

I chose a pair of bright red slippers and tied my hair up in a matching silk scarf.

Twirling around the room, I modeled in front of the mirror.

"What do you think, Stanley?" I asked.

Stanley is my stuffed stegosaurus. He has a long neck and an even longer tail. He also has a great eye for fashion.

Stanley agreed with my choice of outfit and gave me a flattering compliment.

"Why, thank you!" I said, kissing his nose

Then I met my parents at the front door.

As we walked out of our building, Dad took my hand. Mom walked next to me, stroking my hair.

"You know," my dad began, "bullies want attention. They pick on you to make themselves feel better. Have you tried ignoring them?"

"Yes," I said. "They won't stop!"

"Another option," Mom added, "would be to stand up to them. Show them you're not afraid."

"Maybe you're right," I whispered back.

I thought about how brave Claire and Billy were. I didn't think I'd ever be that bold.

I must have been lost in thought because we had walked a couple of blocks before I looked up and noticed my surroundings.

Instantly, I realized where we were going. We were going to the Happy Lucky Golden Dragon, my favorite Chinese restaurant!

"YAY!" I shouted. I ran ahead of my parents and pulled open the door. "What a stupendous surprise! Now, let's eat!"

**

During dinner, Mom and Dad used chopsticks to eat their noodles and fried rice. My chopsticks kept slipping through my fingers.

To be honest, I didn't have the patience to master the art of eating with chopsticks. My food was getting cold! So I picked up my fork and went to town on my vegetable lo mein.

Yes, I'm in fourth grade *and* love vegetables. This shouldn't come as a shock to you. I can also sometimes see the future, remember?

As we ate, I told my parents about the big bake-off at school. I was super excited to work with Claire and Billy, but we still didn't know what we were making.

After we finished our meals, the waiter brought three fortune cookies. That's when Dad started one of his history lectures.

"Did you know that fortune cookies aren't really Chinese?" he said.

Mom and I looked at each other and smiled. We were thinking the same thing . . . here he goes again!

"The exact origin of fortune cookies is unclear," Dad said, "but their recipe is said to be based on a traditional Japanese cracker."

I couldn't wait to break mine open and find the fortune within.

Slipping the small white paper out of the crunchy shell, I smoothed it out and read aloud:

That which you seek has been in front of you all along.

"That which you seek has been in front of you all along."

"That's it!" I shouted, startling my parents. "That's what we'll make for the bake-off!"

"What?" my parents asked.

"Fortune cookies!" I said with a smile.

* * *

The next day was Friday. I waited until lunchtime to make my big announcement.

"What's with all the mystery?" Billy asked.

"Yeah, Krystal," Claire added. "You said you had a surprise for us."

"I do," I said. "Open your palms and close your eyes."

Billy and Claire did as they were told.

I dropped a fortune cookie into each of their hands.

"Ta-da!" I said. "This is what we're going to make for the bake-off. Our very own fortune cookies, filled with our very own fortunes!"

"Ohmygosh, Krystal!" Claire said. "Great idea!"

"I love it too," Billy said.

Suddenly, I felt a shiver up and down my spine. I turned around to find Kate and her entourage standing behind us.

"Oh, Krystal," she said in her fake-nice voice. "The girls and I overheard your idea for the bake-off. Sounds a little stale, don't you think?"

Kate continued to tease us, saying, "My mom is a gourmet chef. She has a blog where she posts pictures of all her fabulous food. She's going to help us make fancy French pastries called crepes."

"Much better than your crusty old fortune cookies," Susan added.

I heard enough. My mother's words were in my head telling me to stand up to Kate. I was inspired to say something clever.

"Here's a prediction," I announced. "No matter how sweet your crepes will be, you three will always be sour creeps!"

Billy and Claire burst into hysterical laughter.

"Way to go, Krystal!" Claire hooted.

Kate gasped, turned red, and stomped away.

Susan and Emily snatched the fortune cookies out of Billy's and Claire's hands before following Kate to the other side of the cafeteria.

"Hey!" Billy shouted. "I was going to eat that!"

"Ah, let them go," I said with newfound confidence. My smile reached from ear to ear. "At least now, Kate and her goons know what kind of competition awaits them."

"Yeah!" Claire agreed. "They're going to get one heck of a fight."

"That trip to the zoo is as good as ours," I said, putting my arms around my friends. "You may rely on it!"

CHAPTER 4

Sweet Dreams

When the final bell rang, Billy, Claire, and I bolted out of the classroom. We couldn't wait for the weekend to start!

Mrs. Voyance, Claire's mom, was waiting for us in the schoolyard. She picks us up on Friday afternoons because the other parents are working.

After a short car ride, Mrs. Voyance dropped Billy and me off at our building. I thanked her and waved good-bye to Claire as they drove away.

"I'm going to visit my mom at work," I said to Billy. I started walking toward the hair salon. "Are you going to join me?"

"Nah," Billy replied. "I'm going to walk to the bakery. Maybe my parents have some day-old doughnuts. They're still good, you know."

I laughed and waved good-bye to Billy.

Through the large display window, I could see my mom and the other hair stylists working on their customers. In my mother's chair was an old woman whose back was turned toward the door.

As I entered the store, I started to get a sensation. I stopped, closed my eyes, and tilted my head. A warm tingle went up and down my body. The same tingle you get when you receive a BIG birthday present and can't wait to open it.

It's totally an amazing feeling.

"Hi, Mom!" I called out.

"Hi, honey," Mom said. "Give me a moment to add the finishing touches on this lovely lady."

SNIP! SNIP! "*Voilà!*" she said.

My mother swiveled the chair around so I could get a good look at the customer.

"GRANDMA!" I shouted with glee.

I ran over and hugged her tightly. She smelled like gardenias and hair spray.

"Hello, darling," Grandma said. "I've been thinking a lot about you."

She stroked my cheek and then cupped my face in her hands.

"Last night, I was sending positive vibes your way," she said. "Did you feel them?"

"I got a vision of you on the Great Wall of China," I said. "And then . . . Dad took us to a Chinese restaurant!"

"Oh, did he?" Grandma asked. There was twinkle in her eye.

I gasped. "Did you send us a mental message?"

"It's part of our gift, my child," Grandma said, kissing my forehead. "Anything is possible if you put your mind to it. Remember that."

"Thanks for the advice, Grandma," I said. Then I remembered, "Gosh! Advice! You'll never guess what my friends and I are doing for the school's annual bake-off!"

"Oh, I'm sure I can," Grandma said, smiling. "But I want you to tell me."

I told her all about the handmade fortune cookies that my group planned to bake. And how we wanted to put handwritten fortunes inside.

Suddenly, my expression changed to a sad one. "I just realized we don't know the first thing about making fortune cookies," I said.

"Cheer up, child," Grandma said. "Good news is always right around the corner."

She nodded her head toward the door.

Just then, Billy ran inside. "Hey, Krystal," he called out. "Guess what?"

"What?" I wondered.

"I asked my parents if we can make our fortune cookies at the bakery, and they said yes!" said Billy. "They have all the latest cooking machinery and stuff. With their help, we're going to blow the competition out of the water."

"Oh, my stars!" I cried. "That's great news!"

"I know, right?" Billy said. "There I was, sneaking around the kitchen looking for a snack, when the idea just popped into my head. Do you believe it?"

Grandma looked at me and winked.

"Without a doubt," I said.

* * *

That evening, Grandma joined us for dinner. After we finished, Dad walked her to the subway so she could get back home to New York City.

Even though she's a quick train ride away, I like to think she's always with me — guiding me like a guardian angel.

Once I changed into my pajamas and brushed my teeth, Mom and Dad came to tuck me in.

"Sweet dreams," they said.

Hugging Stanley tight, I closed my eyes and drifted away to Dreamland . . .

I found myself walking along a winding path through a lush forest on a bright, sunny day. But there was something different about the foliage.

Instead of berries or fruit on the trees, there were gumdrops and candy canes! The bushes around me were tightly coiled strands of rainbow-colored licorice. Tall, swirly lollipops grew out of the ground around me, and the path beneath my feet was made entirely of graham cracker.

I even noticed that the air smelled like pink bubble gum.

A sweet dream indeed, I thought.

Suddenly, something large and white flew by overhead. There was a fluttering of wings and a gust of wind as the mysterious shape landed behind me.

I spun around and gasped.

Before me was the most magnificently majestic creature I had ever seen — a winged unicorn!

"It's a . . . a Pegasus!" I exclaimed.

"Indeed," she replied. "But you can call me Peggy Sue."

"And you can talk!" I said.

"Climb on my back," Peggy Sue urged. "We haven't a moment to lose"

CHAPTER 5

Great Gumdrops!

Without thinking, I did as the Pegasus said. I gripped Peggy Sue's mane tightly, and we soared over the magical candy forest.

"Where are we going?" I asked.

"We must get to Patisserie Palace," Peggy Sue said. "The kingdom is under attack!"

Deafening wind rushed all around me.

"King Sprinkle sent me to find you, Krystal," Peggy Sue replied. "You're our only hope."

"Say what?" I shouted in shock.

The winged horse swooped downward toward a large castle made entirely of cake, glazed with strawberry frosting. The towers were waffled ice cream cones with spires made of whipped cream and giant cherries on top.

All around the castle was a bubbling, swirling milk shake moat. It looked so delicious!

"We've arrived, young hero," Peggy Sue stated.

"Uh," I stammered. "What did you mean I'm your only hope?"

"Only you possess the strength to defeat the dragon," said the unicorn.

"D-d-dragon?" I gulped.

"Yes!" Peggy Sue exclaimed. "That monster has set her fiery sights on King Sprinkle's crown. She will stop at nothing until she rules the kingdom."

Peggy Sue closed her eyes, and the horn atop her forehead started to glow.

"Great gumdrops!" she cried, pointing a hoof toward the sky. "The dragon is upon us. Look!"

A scaly beast with sharp jagged teeth appeared above us. The dragon flapped her mighty wings and circled the castle. Her scales shimmered orange and yellow in the sunlight.

"ROOAAAR!"

The dragon belched a fireball at one of the waffle cone towers. The structure went up in smoke, turning into a toasted crumbling mess.

This caused the enormous dollop of whipped cream resting on top of it to come tumbling down. The cream slid down the frosted castle wall. It grew into an unstoppable avalanche of delicious danger. And it was coming right at us!

Peggy Sue took flight, and I hugged her neck for dear life. We swerved and swooped, but weren't fast enough to avoid the avalanche.

PLOP-POW!

We were being dragged down toward the depths of the milk shake moat.

Peggy Sue flapped her wings, but it was useless. The sugary sweetness washed over us.

Everything went dark.

***

Gasping for breath, I woke up and found my pillow over my head. I had been chewing on it in my sleep. There was a big glob of slobber and drool all over it. Gross!

"Whoa, what a dream," I said aloud.

I climbed out of bed and picked up Stanley off the floor.

"I don't know what you think," I told him, "but that certainly felt like a sign for caution."

Stanley stared back at me. He agreed.

I looked over at my alarm clock.

"Great galaxies!" I exclaimed. "Today is the day. I'm meeting Claire and Billy at the House of Sweets to make our fortune cookies."

I quickly rummaged through the closet and dresser to find a truly spectacular baking outfit.

"Aha!" I exclaimed lifting a T-shirt in the air. It had an illustration of a chocolate chip cookie on the front with the phrase "'That's the way the cookie crumbles!" written in swirly type.

"How appropriate," I said. "This is the one!"

I wriggled myself into a pair of polka-dot leggings that looked like chocolate chips and topped off the outfit with a matching scarf.

I was ready to bake in style!

As I headed into the kitchen, I passed Mom and Dad in the hallway. They were still rubbing the sleep from their eyes.

Moments later, while I was eating my cereal at the table, I got a tingling sensation. My spoon stopped in midair, dripping milk.

I closed my eyes and tilted my head.

"It's Billy," I said.

"It's Billy what?" my father asked, yawning.

Knock. Knock. Knock.

"It's Billy at the door," I said.

I hopped out of my chair and opened the door. Billy was wearing a baker's apron over his clothes and a white chef's hat.

"*Bonjour!*" He greeted us. "What's cooking, good-looking?"

"Billy!" I said, blushing. "What are you saying?"

"I don't know," he shrugged. "That's what my dad says to my mom."

"We're going to the bakery to work on our project," I told my parents. "See you later!"

"Hold on," Dad said. "I'll walk you over and pick up some coffee to help us wake up."

"Shake a leg, Mr. Ball," Billy told him. "Time waits for no man!"

"Ooh, I like that," I said. "That can be one of the fortunes we write in our cookies."

"Ha!" Billy laughed. "Then this is going to be a piece of cake. I've got thousands of them."

"Speaking of cake," I said to Billy. "Wait until you hear about the dream I had last night. I think it's a bad sign of things that will happen today."

"Well, if it involves cake," he said, "then the outlook must be good."

Maybe Billy's right, I thought, *but then why do I feel like something will go wrong?*

CHAPTER 6

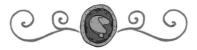

Recipe for Disaster

On our way to the House of Sweets, we met Claire and Mrs. Voyance on the corner. Together, we entered the store. It smelled amazing.

The bakery had long, glass display windows with pastries galore. Sweets and treats stretched as far as the eye could see: cupcakes, tarts, croissants, muffins, cakes, biscuits, turnovers, and pies, oh, my!

I'm salivating just thinking about the sight.

Billy's parents were busy rushing from customer to customer. When his dad had a free moment, Mr. Katsikis brought us into the kitchen.

"Welcome to my magic workshop," he announced. "Are you excited to be here?"

Claire and I admired the kitchen. "This is so cool," I exclaimed.

"I'll return when the breakfast rush slows down to help you," Mr. Katsikis said. "Please, don't burn the place down!" He eyed Billy and left.

Everything gleamed with a metallic sheen. There were big tools for kneading and mixing dough hanging from the wall and trays of pastries fresh out of the oven next to more trays ready to go in. The smell was sweet and tasty.

"MMMMmmm . . ." I said, licking my lips.

As I reached for a fresh, gooey, chocolate chip cookie, Billy swatted my hand away.

"Don't eat anything," Billy warned. "My dad has eyes everywhere."

"Okay, gang," said Claire. "Let's concentrate and come up with some fortunes."

We went and sat at an empty counter. Claire opened her notebook to a fresh sheet of paper.

I took out my pink gel pen from my backpack. It was decorated with swirly glitter and had a fuzzy yellow star at the top.

"Isn't that your inspiration pen?" Billy asked.

"Why, yes," I replied. "And it will help us come up with fabulous fortunes."

I rubbed my chin and stared at the pen.

"Marvelous moonbeams!" I cried. "I've got a good one!"

"Okay, Ball," Billy said. "Let's hear it!"

"Always follow your dreams," I answered and wrote it down.

"That's a good one," said Claire. "My turn . . ."

She thought for a sec.

"Got it!" she exclaimed. "You are a star — don't forget to shine."

I clapped my hands and smiled.

"Ooh, ooh, I have one," Billy said. "Don't pick on your sister when she's holding a baseball bat!'"

Claire and I exchanged looks. "Huh?" we said.

"Live and learn," Billy replied. He leaned forward to show us a bump the size of a golf ball on the top of his head. "Wish I had a fortune keep me out of that misfortune."

We laughed and continued coming up with more sayings. When we finished, each one was cut up into a strip of paper.

Mr. Katsikis entered the kitchen. He was holding aprons for Claire and me.

"Okay, my junior bakers," he said. "Let's get cooking."

Moments later, we had gathered our ingredients and laid them out on the table. Claire and I measured a half cup of flour, a half a cup of sugar, and a teaspoon of vanilla.

Billy cracked open two eggs and separated the yolks out.

Then we mixed them all up in a bowl to create our cookie batter.

"Now we must preheat the oven to four hundred degrees," Mr. Katsikis told us.

Billy jumped up. "I'll do that!" he yelled.

He ran over to the oven and turned the giant knob on the side.

"Initiating . . . preheating . . . sequence!" Billy said in his robot voice.

"Next we lightly coat a baking sheet with cooking spray," instructed Mr. Katsikis.

"Ooh, I want to do that!" I said.

After Claire finished mixing the cookie batter, we spooned out four dollops and placed them near each corner of the baking sheet. Then we repeated that for the next tray.

We filled five baking sheets for our first batch.

"Okay, that's it," Billy's dad said. "Now we put them in the oven for about five minutes."

The wait seemed like an eternity!

Finally, the oven dinged, signaling our cookies were ready.

Mr. Katsikis put on oven mitts and removed the piping hot trays. Once they cooled off a bit, we placed a fortune in the middle of each cookie. Then we folded them in half, pressing the very top edges together lightly.

"Watch this," said Billy's dad.

He gently pulled the ends of the cookie over the rim of a clean mixing bowl.

"Keep them here until they cool and dry," he said. "That way they will curve into the fortune cookie shape."

"Wow, that was easy," I said.

"What did I tell you?" Billy said. "Piece of cake!"

We completed the second batch and prepped them for the oven.

After he put them in, Mr. Katsikis got called away by Mrs. Katsikis, leaving us alone.

"We have five minutes to kill before they're done," I said.

"Are you thinking what I'm thinking?" Billy asked.

I closed my eyes, tilted my head, and an idea popped in.

"As I see it, yes," I replied smiling.

The three of us shouted, "Paranormal Investigators!"

CHAPTER 7

Sticky Situation

"BRAINS!!" Billy shouted.

He had opened a can of apple filling and scooped up two handfuls of the gooey stuff. It slid through his fingers.

"BRAINS!" Billy said, licking up the filling.

Then he reached over and wiped his hands on Claire's apron.

"Ahhh!" she screamed. "I've been slimed!"

She slumped to the ground gasping for air.

Grabbing a whisk off the counter, I ran to Claire's side saying, "Have no fear, I am here! I will stop this creature with my Zombie Zapper."

Pointing the utensil at Billy, I shouted, "ZAP! ZAP! BLAM!"

"BLURGH!" Billy gurgled and crawled under one of the tables.

I turned my attention to Claire. Her eyes were closed, and she was lying on her side.

"Speak to me," I cried, giving her a shake.

"BRAINS!" Claire shouted. She jerked her body toward me with outstretched arms. "BRAINS!"

"Not you too!" I moaned.

I aimed my Zombie Zapper at her, but she slapped it out of my hand. I turned to run after it, but Billy surprised me. He threw cherry filling on my apron that left a big red splatter.

"I've been hit!" I yelled, clutching my chest. "What will happen now?"

"BRAINS!" Billy shouted.

"BRAINS!" shouted Claire, grabbing my Zombie Zapper.

As they shuffled closer, my back came up against the wall. I was trapped.

"Please don't eat my precious brains!" I wailed.

DING!

The oven timer rang. The cookies were ready!

"That was fast," I said. "I guess time flies when you're having fun."

"Hey," said Claire. "That sounds like a good fortune to me. Let's put it in our cookies."

"Totally," I replied.

As we ran toward the oven, I slipped on a patch of apple filling on the floor. Stumbling forward, I knocked into Claire, who fell onto Billy, who crashed into a large vat of vanilla icing.

The tub teetered and tottered and tipped over, spilling vanilla icing everywhere. SPLOOSH!

"Oh, no!" we cried.

The icing splashed onto our shoes, the counter, and spread across the tile toward the oven.

The three of us tumbled on top of each other on the slippery floor. We were completely covered from head to toe with icing.

"This sure is a sticky situation," Billy said.

I started to giggle, but then a shiver went up and down my spine.

"You guys, something like this happened in my dream," I said.

I told my friends what I had seen last night and how I thought it was a sign of caution.

"It so totally was a sign," added Claire.

Suddenly, the smoke alarm blared.

BREEP! BREEP! BREEP!

"Our cookies are burning!" I screamed.

Mr. Katsikis burst into the room. "What's going on here?" he bellowed.

He walked carefully to the oven and turned on an overhead fan. Then he opened the oven door. Black clouds of smoke billowed out, getting sucked into the fan.

Mrs. Katsikis ran in and turned off the smoke detector. Then she took in the sight.

"Oh my," was all she could muster.

Billy's father glared at us, and I felt a sharp pang of guilt.

"Mr. and Mrs. Katsikis," I started, "I'm so sorry. I'll help clean everything up right now."

"That's very thoughtful," Mrs. Katsikis told us. "But I think it's best if you all go home."

She ushered us out the kitchen door into the front of the shop. I craned my neck back to look at Billy, but he was staring at the ground.

My head was spinning so fast that before I knew it, I was standing outside the House of Sweets with Claire at my side.

"Uh-oh," she said. "This is so not good."

"I know," I whispered back.

"What are we going to do?" she asked me. "Billy's in trouble, but we're all to blame. Plus, our good fortune cookies are still in the kitchen. How are we going to make any money and go to the zoo? How are we going to beat the Mean Team?"

Claire was absolutely right. Everything was going wrong, and I felt sick. I shut my eyes and tilted my head.

Maybe I can catch a glimpse of the future, I thought. But nothing appeared.

I opened my eyes and looked at my best friend.

"Outlook hazy," I answered. "Cannot predict now."

CHAPTER 8

The Cookie Crumbles

After the fortune cookie fiasco at the House of Sweets, Claire and I ended up at my apartment. When my parents saw how upset we were, they asked us what happened. So, I told them.

"Oh, honey," Mom said. "That's terrible."

"Chin up, sweetheart. Your mother and I can help make more cookies right here," Dad offered.

"Of course," Mom said cheerfully. "I'm sure we can find a recipe on the Internet."

Dad brought over his laptop computer and started searching for recipes.

I saw how excited my parents were, but inside I still felt uneasy. Don't get me wrong — Mom and Dad are great cooks, but they're not bakers.

Dad saw my pained expression.

"Don't worry, Krystal," he said, "this batch is going to be the best one yet."

"How hard can it be?" Mom asked.

I forced a smile.

My parents found a recipe online and skimmed through it. Mom said, "Perfect! We have all the ingredients right here!"

And so, we started from scratch.

Soon after the new batter was ready, Claire and I lined the cookie trays and placed them in the preheated oven. We set the timer and waited.

Once the batch was cooked, we put them on the counter to dry, folding the hot dough over the mixing bowl to get the fortune cookie shape.

"There, that wasn't so hard, was it?" Dad asked.

The fortune cookies did look good, after all.

I smiled for real and said, "Thanks, Daddy!"

Finally, when the cookies had cooled, Claire and I picked a couple up to try them.

"Ew!" I cried. "The dough is soggy and mushy. Not at all crunchy like it should be."

Dad scratched his head, saying, "Hmm, we did everything the recipe asked . . . I don't understand."

"Here's a fortune," I said. "Eat these cookies if you want to get sick."

"Krystal!" my mother said, sharply.

I stormed out of the kitchen and plopped onto the sofa. My hopes of winning the bake-off went up in smoke back at the House of Sweets.

Claire sat next to me. "It's all going to be fine, Krystal," she offered.

Suddenly, there was a knock at the door. My mom opened it. Billy was standing there holding a bakery box and looking bummed.

"Here are the cookies that survived," he said. "At least *you* can sell something."

"What do you mean, *you*?" I asked.

"I have to go the bakery every day after school and scrub the floor until it stops sticking to our shoes," Billy told us. "Starting tomorrow."

"But the bake-off is tomorrow!" I cried.

"I know," he said glumly. "I can't make it."

"Well, this stinks!" Claire exclaimed. "Our team is falling apart."

My ears perked up. I looked down at the writing on my shirt and read it out loud.

"That's the way the cookie crumbles," I said. "It was a sign all along."

***

That night, after Billy and Claire went home, I sat alone on my bed. Stanley was by my side.

Placed out in front of me were my crystal ball, tarot cards, and tea leaves. These objects helped guide my gift, as Grandma called it. Right now, I was drawing a blank. I couldn't see anything.

Flopping onto my pillow, I stared at my ceiling. All across it were glow-in-the-dark star stickers.

"Oh, my stars!" I gasped. "That's it!"

Dad told me that during ancient times, sailors used the stars as maps to guide them on their ocean travels.

"I should use the stars to guide me," I said.

Grabbing Stanley, I hopped out of bed, slid on my slippers, and padded down the hall.

"Where are you off to, honey?" Dad asked as I passed him.

"To the roof!" I exclaimed.

I climbed the stairs to get to the roof of our building. Sometimes, Billy, Claire, and I would go up there and play. It was the perfect place for us to have our secret headquarters. Plus, the view was amazing. You could look out over Queens and see the Manhattan skyline. Anyone up there felt as if they were on top of the world!

Hidden in the corner, behind a potted fern, was my trusty satchel. In it I kept my telescope case and an old astronomy textbook that Dad brought home from his school's bookstore.

I put Stanley down on the table and picked up my satchel. "Let's see if the stars give me any bright ideas, Stanley."

While I was constructing the telescope, Mom and Dad joined me on the roof.

"We figured you could use some company, and a sweet treat," Mom said, holding a mug of cocoa.

"Thanks, Mom," I said and hugged her.

As I sipped the delicious drink, Dad set up my telescope on the ledge and peered through it.

"What are we looking for, Krystal?" he asked.

I shrugged. "I thought maybe the stars could guide me. Show me what the future holds."

Using the telescope, I scanned the starry night sky. Finally, I found an interesting cluster. Three stars formed a triangle, and there were a number of stars that extended from it, in crooked lines out from under it.

I described the constellation to my parents.

"Hmm," Dad said, rubbing his chin. "Let's consult the guide." He flipped through the textbook and settled on a spread.

"Is this what you see?" he asked.

"Yes!" I exclaimed.

I read the constellation's name — and gasped.

"PEGASUS!"

"Pegasus was the winged horse that helped heroes like Perseus and Bellerophon defeat many monsters that plagued the cities of ancient Greece," my father read aloud.

"Wow, cool!" Mom said. Then she saw I was lost deep in thought. "What is it, honey?"

"I dreamed of Pegasus last night," I said.

I placed the mug of cocoa on the table and picked up Stanley.

"I'm going to bed," I said. "There are still some monsters I need to take care of, here in the real world and in dreamland."

"You're a funny kid, you know that?" Dad said.

"Yeah, I know," I said and smiled.

Mom kissed me on the cheek. "Have a good night," she said. "See you in the morning."

I put two fingers next to my temple and acted like I was having a vision. "Not if I see you first!"

CHAPTER 9

The Dragon Returns

Immediately after I fell asleep, I found myself back on the graham cracker drawbridge of Patisserie Palace. Peggy Sue was by my side, shaking whipped cream out of her feathers.

I looked down and saw the rest of the cream swirling around inside the milk shake moat.

"Wow, Peggy Sue!" I exclaimed. "How did we escape the avalanche?"

"We have Serina to thank for that," she replied.

"Who?" I asked.

"Me, of course," said a lovely voice.

I turned to see a glamorous mermaid with a shimmering tail sitting along the moat's bank.

"Peggy Sue is a dear friend of mine," Serina stated. "So I rushed to the rescue as soon as I got word there was trouble."

"Who told you?" I asked.

"My fine, finny friends!" Serina said, pointing down.

Red, green, and yellow Swedish fish splashed through the milk shake waves. Behind them, a school of Goldfish crackers swam by.

At that moment, there was a thunderous roar.

GROOOAAR!

The dangerous dragon had returned.

"That beast needs to be taught a lesson!" I said.

"And you are the teacher," Peggy Sue told me. "Here are your supplies."

The winged horse produced a sugar-coated satchel. Inside were a helmet and chest-plate made of hard candy shell, a swirly lollipop shield, and a long licorice lasso.

"Hurry, child," Peggy Sue said. "Put these on!"

As I rushed to dress myself, the dragon swooped down toward us.

There was another deafening roar, and a blazing fireball blasted the bridge. The graham cracker crumbled beneath our feet. Embers hit the waffle cone tower and FWOOSH!

It burst into flames.

Serina raised her arms, causing waves of milk shake to lurch out of the moat. The cool, thick liquid landed on the wall, dousing the blaze.

"Climb on my back," Peggy Sue said.

Together we flew up toward the dragon. The scaly creature belched another fireball at us.

Peggy Sue swerved under the blast and then zoomed back up. I was face to face with our foe.

With newfound strength, I twirled the licorice lasso over my head and let it loose. The loop coiled around the dragon's snout, tying it tight.

"That's enough out of you," I scolded. "Keep that trap shut!"

Defeated, the dragon flew away.

Peggy whooped with glee. "Way to tell that big buzzard to buzz off!"

Together, we landed on a turret made of toffee.

"The kingdom is saved!" said a powerful voice.

King Sprinkle appeared before us. He was a short round man with brown hair and a long beard. His royal wardrobe, from his long purple cape to his pointed shoes, was covered with rainbow-colored sprinkles.

"Your majesty," Peggy Sue said, bowing her head. "We are at your service."

"No, it is I who is at your service, my dears," King Sprinkle replied, bowing his head in return.

Then he turned and looked down over the side of the turret. I followed his gaze and saw Serina. Surrounding her were all the kingdom's inhabitants.

"All hail Krystal Ball," the king announced. "Protector of Patisserie Palace!"

Everyone erupted into an enormous cheer. The royal subjects started chanting my name.

"Krystal! Krystal! Krystal!"

I was going to burst with joy.

That was when I heard a loud voice shout, "Krystal, WAKE UP!"

* * *

I jolted upright and looked around. I was in my bedroom, and my mother stood over me.

"Krystal, dear, you're going to be late for school," she said.

"Suffering solar systems!" I exclaimed.

Frazzled, I leaped out of bed and rushed to get ready.

Several minutes later, I walked into my classroom, carrying the box with our precious fortune cookies inside.

Miss Callisto clapped her hands. "Attention, class. Put all your baked items on the table in the back. The bake-off will take place at the end of the day in the cafeteria. Oh, I'm so excited!"

Throughout the day, I looked up at the clock. It just dragged on forever!

Finally, class was over and the time for the bake-off arrived. Unfortunately, Billy had to go to the bakery and clean up our mess.

"I'll catch you later," he said sadly. "Good luck!"

Claire and I waved good-bye and headed to the cafeteria with our fortune cookies. There was a big banner that said Nikola Tesla Elementary School Annual Bake-Off.

The tables were set up in a circle, and we found ours all the way in the back. "I guess they're saving the best for last, huh?" Claire said, smiling. "I'll go get a tablecloth. BRB!"

As I headed to the table, Kate appeared and blocked my path. Her table was next to ours. Ugh!

She was carrying a silver serving platter with a domed cover. I hated to admit it, but whatever was inside smelled really delicious. Like bananas and chocolate.

Kate looked down and scoffed. "Is that your excuse for an entry? It's sad. Like you," she said.

My faced burned, but I stood firm and said, "Not as sad as you, Kate. You make people feel bad so you can feel good about yourself."

"Nobody talks to me that way!" she shrieked. "I'm Kate Saxon!"

"No, you're just a big bully," I said.

I walked passed Kate feeling like the hero from my dream, that I had just defeated the dragon all over again. Sadly, my victory was short lived.

Kate stuck out her foot and tripped me.

I stumbled forward, dropping the box. The fortune cookies skidded across the floor.

Adding to my misfortune, a bunch of boys came trampling by. They accidentally crushed and crunched and kicked the cookies around.

Everything we had created was destroyed!

Kate really was like the fire-breathing dragon.

"You rotten reptile!" I shouted.

She flipped her hair and walked away.

Claire saw me on my knees and rushed over.

"Oh no!" she gasped. "What happened?"

I told her the whole story.

Claire balled her fists. "I'm going to march over there and knock her block off!"

"Forget it," I cried. "What are we going to do?"

"I don't know," Claire answered. "It's not like we can magically make more out of thin air."

Suddenly, I had a revelation. I remembered what Grandma said at the salon: "Anything is possible if you put your mind to it."

"Actually, Claire," I said to her. "I think we can!"

CHAPTER 10

The Sweetest Treat

"Quick, Claire," I urged. "We need to get in touch with Billy!"

"How?" she asked. "We don't have cell phones."

"I had something else in mind."

I closed my eyes and took a deep breath. I remembered that Grandma had reached out and influenced me with a vision. I tried to picture Billy at the House of Sweets. An image soon appeared. Billy was standing in the kitchen mopping.

Hello, Billy, can you hear me? I said in my mind.

In the vision, Billy stopped mopping and looked around confused. Then he stuck a finger in his ear, cleaning it out.

It's me, Krystal!

Billy dropped the mop.

"K-Krystal?" he stammered. "Where are you?"

I'm in your mind!

"Ah!" he screamed, grabbing his head. "Get out of there!"

Relax, Billy. I'm sending you a mental message. Claire and I need your help!

I told him everything.

Can you and your dad whip up another batch of fortune cookies really quick?

"I'll do my best," he said.

I opened my eyes and said to Claire, "Cross your fingers and hope Billy comes through."

At that moment, Principal Nova entered the cafeteria with another well-dressed woman.

The principal approached the podium, and the room quieted.

"Your attention, please! This year, I've brought a very special guest judge to help me find a winner," she said, and the other woman waved.

"Mildred and I went to elementary school together and have stayed best friends ever since," continued the principal. "She went on to become a famous celebrity chef, and we're lucky to have her here today. Allow me to present, Millie Fay!"

The cafeteria applauded.

Claire clasped her hands and sighed. "Gosh, she's so great! My parents watch her TV show every morning."

Right then, Miss Callisto walked over to our table and saw the mess.

"What happened here, girls?" she asked.

"Well, I, uh, I don't know," I stuttered.

"*Kate* did it!" Claire blurted out. "She sabotaged us!"

"Claire, that is a serious accusation," Miss Callisto sternly stated.

"It's true," said a voice.

It was Emily's.

"Kate tripped Krystal," she said, looking at us. "I watched it happen. I'm sorry."

Miss Callisto asked Kate about the incident.

Kate turned red and hollered, "Don't listen to them — they're all liars!"

Susan came to Emily's defense. Kate was angry at the betrayal of her friends.

Before she could say anything, Miss Callisto spoke. "In light of your group's confession, I'm afraid the only fair option is to disqualify you from the competition. I will not tolerate cheaters, Ms. Saxon, do you understand?"

Kate grumbled a reply. Then she ran out of the room, crying.

Miss Callisto left to inform Principal Nova and Millie Fay about the recent events.

"Um, I guess we should thank you," I said to Emily and Susan. "But why did you help us out?"

Emily pulled out a slip of paper and handed it to me.

"Remember when we stole those cookies from you?" Emily said. "Well, this was inside one."

I took the slip and read it aloud: "You can catch more flies with honey than with vinegar."

"I asked my mom what it meant. She said it's easier to get what you want by being polite to them than by making demands. I guess the same goes for making friends and being popular," Emily told us. "We're sorry for being so mean."

"Whoa! Beware the awesome power of the fortune cookie," Claire said.

And as simply as that, the tension between us had broken.

I realized that winning the bake-off didn't matter. It was more important to make peace with two of the Mean Team members and spread positive energy between us.

Seconds later, Billy entered the cafeteria with his father. They were still wearing aprons and holding a new batch of fortune cookies.

Billy found us in the crowd and hurried over.

"Sorry we're late. I tried to bake them as fast as I could," he said. "Did the judges come by yet?"

"No, you're just in time!" I replied. "The judges are right there."

"Is that who I think it is?" Mr. Katsikis said, looking at the celebrity chef. "Oh my goodness!"

Principal Nova and Millie Fay approached our table. They each tried one of our cookies.

"Mmm," said Principal Nova. "These are delicious!"

Claire, Billy, and I were happy, but it Mr. Katsikis who was grinning from ear to ear. He looked like the Cheshire Cat.

Millie Fay added, "They are crunchy, sweet, and . . . somewhat familiar. Where did you find this recipe?"

"From your book!" Mr. Katsikis exclaimed. "I'm your biggest fan!"

And like a magician, he pulled the *Millie Fay Cookbook* out of his apron.

Millie Fay laughed and said, "Oh my, you certainly are!"

"Please honor me with your autograph. Oh and a picture, if you don't mind."

Mr. Katsikis handed his phone to Billy, who snapped a picture with its camera.

"Thank you, Ms. Fay," Mr. Katsikis said. "My wife will be in shock. She's a big fan too. I think she loves you more than me!"

The celebrity chef blushed.

"One question," said Principal Nova. "If these are fortune cookies, where are the fortunes?"

The three of us gulped.

"Well, you see, this is what happened," Claire started, but Billy interrupted.

"We, uh, wanted to be fair and give everyone the same fortune. Right, Krystal?"

I looked at Billy and Claire and Susan and Emily. Then it hit me.

"Our fortune," I told them, "is that true friendship is the sweetest treat of all!"

Principal Nova, Miss Callisto, and Millie Fay clapped their hands.

"Well, I don't know about you, ladies, but this group has my vote." Millie Fay said. "Plus, I plan on buying all these fortune cookies and making a hefty donation to the school!"

"That's wonderful news," Principal Nova said to us. "Congratulations! You are the winners, and you'll all be going to the Bronx Zoo!"

Billy, Claire, and I jumped for joy.

"Woohoo!" we cried and slapped high fives.

The principal and chef shook our hands and headed to the podium to make the announcement.

"Wow," Claire said. "We totally pulled it off. I can't believe it!"

"Was there ever any doubt?" Billy asked.

"Well, my dreams did show many ups and downs, but it all balanced out in the end." I said.

"We make an amazing team," Claire replied, hugging us close.

"Thanks to Krystal's amazing gift," Billy added.

"You're absolutely right," I said. "After all, being a small medium is such a ball!"

Ruby Ann Phillips

Ruby Ann Phillips is the pseudonym of a *New York Times* best-selling author who lives in the Big Apple, in a neighborhood much like Krystal Ball's.

Sernur Isik

Sernur Isik lives in magical Istanbul, Turkey. As a child, she loved drawing fairies and unicorns, as well as wonderful, imaginative scenes of her home country. Since graduating from the Fine Arts Faculty-Graphic Design of Ataturk University, Sernur has worked as a professional illustrator and artist for children's books, mascot designs, and textile brands. She likes collecting designer toys, reading books, and traveling the world.

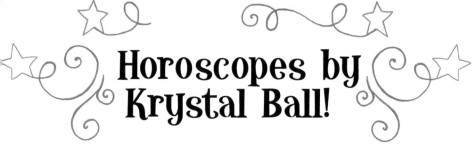

Horoscopes by Krystal Ball!

Astrologists believe a diagram of the position of stars and planets on a person's birthday fortells the future. This diagram is divided into twelve groups called *signs*. Find your sign and Krystal's prediction for your future!

ARIES (MAR 21–APR 19)
Krystal says: "You're always willing to tackle new adventures, but be careful not to rush into things too quickly!"
Lucky numbers: 9, 15, 33

TAURUS (APR 20–MAY 20)
Krystal says: "There's some change coming soon. You may want things to say the same, but don't worry. Change can be a good thing!"
Lucky numbers: 2, 18, 49

GEMINI (MAY 21–JUN 21)
Krystal says: "Your laugh is contagious, and you have a great sense of humor. So embrace your jokester side, Gemini, and spread smiles!"
Lucky numbers: 1, 24, 91

CANCER (JUN 22–JUL 22)
Krystal says: "Don't be afraid to work hard for what you want. Go for a goal! You're commitment will be rewarded."
Lucky numbers: 6, 21, 75

LEO (JUL 23–AUG 22)
Krystal says: "Leo, have you been feeling lonely? Organize a picnic for you and your friends and be the social butterfly that you are!"
Lucky numbers: 12, 53, 67

VIRGO (AUG 23–SEP 22)
Krystal says: "You may not be the loudest of your friends, but you've got a lot to say! Jump into the conversation and give your opinion."
Lucky numbers: 14, 36, 42

LIBRA (SEP 23–OCT 22)

Krystal says: "Everyone can use a little encouragement now and then. Do something nice for someone today!"
Lucky numbers: 4, 27, 83

SCORPIO (OCT 23–NOV 21)

Krystal says: "You love being independent, but don't be afraid to ask for help. Friends and family got your back!"
Lucky numbers: 3, 31, 62

SAGITTARIUS (NOV 22–DEC 21)

Krystal says: "Itching for something new, Sagittarius? Try learning a new sport or a new instrument just for fun!"
Lucky numbers: 19, 25, 64

CAPRICORN (DEC 22–JAN19)

Krystal says: "Your imagination could use some exercise lately! Let your creativity run free."
Lucky numbers: 15, 37, 80

AQUARIUS (JAN 20–FEB 18)

Krystal says: "You love giving advice, but listen to what others are saying. You may hear some words of wisdom."
Lucky numbers: 7, 38, 95

PISCES (FEB 19–MAR 20)

Krystal says: Looking for a new creative activity, Pisces? Try decorating some cupcakes. They'll look perfectly pretty!"
Lucky numbers: 20, 41, 73

Krystal's Fortune Game!

What you'll need:

- Markers, crayons, or colored pencils
- A square piece of paper
- One or more friends!

1. First, fold your square piece of paper diagonally in half to make a triangle. Make sure there is a crease. Then, open it up again.

2. Fold the paper diagonally the opposite way to make a second triangle. When you open the paper up again, there should be two creases in the shape of an X.

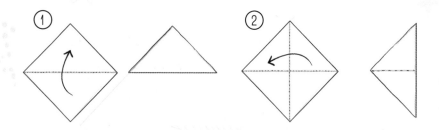

3. Next, take one corner of your paper and fold it toward the center. Repeat with each corner of the square. All the corners should meet in the center of the square.

4. Flip over the paper so that the folded side is facedown.

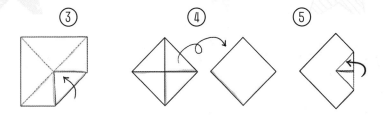

5. Repeat steps 3 and 4 to make a smaller square.

6. Keep the fortune-teller folded side up and write the numbers 1–8 in each of the creased triangles. There should be only one number in each triangle.

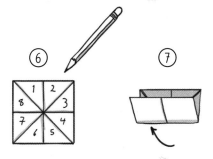

7. Open each flap and write a fortune on the inside of each triangle. You should have two fortunes written inside each flap.

8. Close the flaps back up, and flip the fortune-teller over. Now color each of the four squares a different color. Once you've colored them in, you're ready to predict the future!

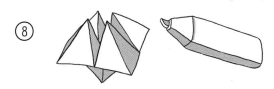

See what the future holds for . . .

Krystal ★Ball★

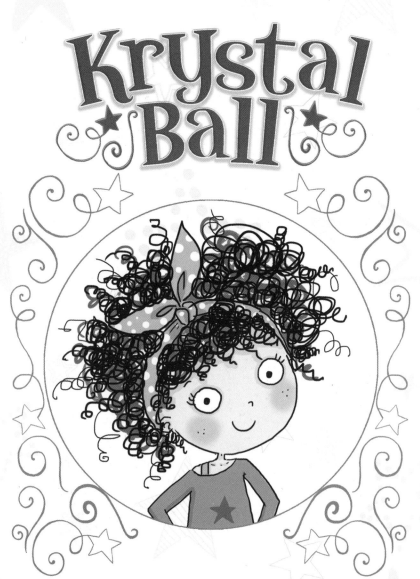

Read another book to find out!

Available from Picture Window Books
www.capstoneyoungreaders.com

THE FUN DOESN'T STOP HERE!

Discover more at www.capstonekids.com

Videos & Contests/Games & Puzzles
Friends & Favorites/Authors & Illustrators

Find cool websites and more books like this one at www.facthound.com.
Just type in the Book ID: 9781479558742 and you are ready to go!